BoCo

Based on *The Railway Series* by the Rev. W. Awdry

Illustrations by
Clive Spong and Jerry Smith

EGMONT

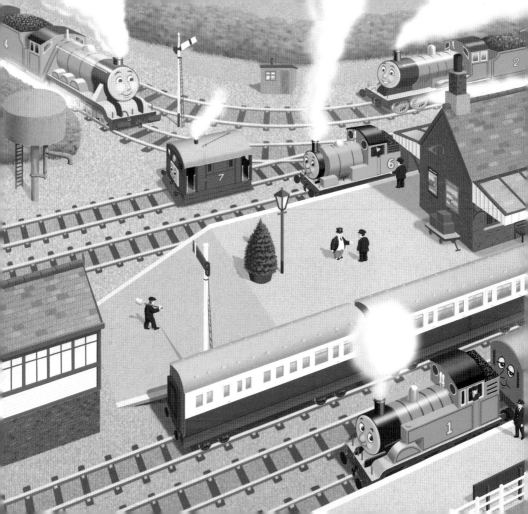

EGMONT

We bring stories to life

First published in Great Britain in 2008
by Egmont UK Limited
239 Kensington High Street, London W8 6SA

Thomas the Tank Engine & Friends™

CREATED BY BRITT ALLCROFT

Based on the Railway Series by the Reverend W Awdry
© 2008 Gullane (Thomas) LLC. A HIT Entertainment company.
Thomas the Tank Engine & Friends and Thomas & Friends are trademarks of Gullane (Thomas) Limited.
Thomas the Tank Engine & Friends and Design is Reg. U.S. Pat. & Tm. Off.

HiT entertainment

ISBN 978 1 4052 3784 0
3 5 7 9 10 8 6 4 2
Printed in Italy

The Forest Stewardship Council (FSC) is an international, non-governmental organisation
dedicated to promoting responsible management of the world's forests. FSC operates a
system of forest certification and product labelling that allows consumers to identify
wood and wood-based products from well-managed forests.

For more information about Egmont's paper-buying policy please visit www.egmont.co.uk/ethicalpublishing

For more information about the FSC please visit their website at www.fsc.org

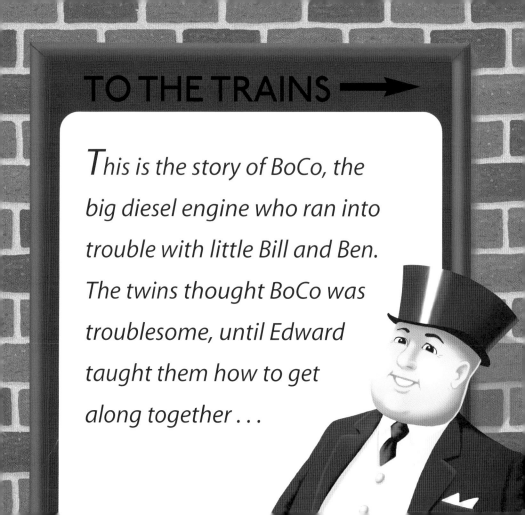

*T*his is the story of BoCo, the big diesel engine who ran into trouble with little Bill and Ben. The twins thought BoCo was troublesome, until Edward taught them how to get along together . . .

Bill and Ben are twin tank engines, who live at a port on Edward's line.

Each has four wheels, a tiny chimney and dome and a small, squat cab.

Wherever Bill goes, Ben goes too.

They are kept busy pulling trucks for ships in the Harbour and engines on the Main Line.

The trucks are filled with China Clay dug from nearby hills. The Clay is used to make pottery, paper, paint, plastics and many other things.

One morning, Bill and Ben shunted their trucks into a line, then went to collect some more. But when they got back, the trucks were gone.

Bill and Ben were most surprised.

Their Drivers examined a patch of oil. "That's a diesel," they said, wiping the rails clean.

"It's a what'll?" asked Bill.

"A diseasel, I think he said," replied Ben.

"There's a notice about diseasels in our shed. It says, 'coughs and sneezels spread diseasels'!" said Bill.

"You had a cough in your smokebox yesterday," said Ben. "It's your fault the diseasel came!"

"My Fireman cleaned it, it's not my fault, it's yours!" Bill snorted back.

"Stop arguing, you two," laughed their Drivers. "Let's go and rescue our trucks."

Bill and Ben were worried.

"The diseasel will magic us away like our trucks!" cried Ben.

"He won't magic us," Bill's Driver told them, "we'll more likely magic him."

Their Drivers were clever and thought of a plan. "The diesel doesn't know you're twins. We'll take away your names and numbers and then this is what we'll do . . ." they said.

So, puffing hard, the twins set off to find the diesel. They were looking forward to playing tricks on him.

Slowly and carefully, they puffed into Edward's Yard. The diesel was on a siding with the missing trucks.

Ben hid behind, but Bill puffed boldly alongside.

Bill pretended to be frightened. "You're a big bully," he whimpered. "You'll be sorry."

He ran back and hid behind the trucks on the other side, as Ben puffed forward.

"Truck stealer!" hissed Ben.

He steamed away, then Bill took his place. This went on and on till the poor diesel's eyes nearly popped out.

"Stop! You're making me giddy," moaned the diesel engine.

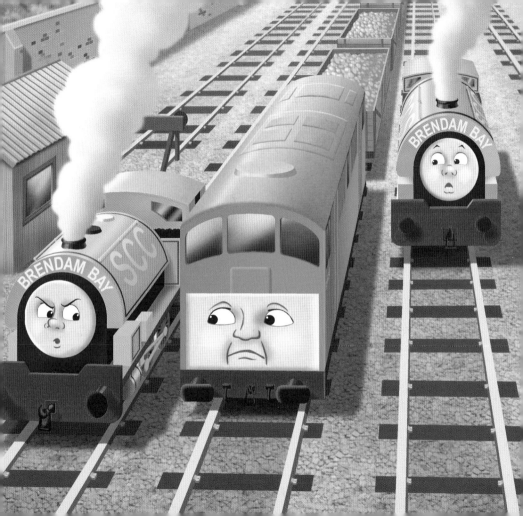

The two engines stopped, and puffed forwards together.

"Are there two of you?" asked the diesel.

"Yes, we're twins," said Bill.

"I might have known it!" huffed the diesel engine.

Just then, Edward the Blue Engine bustled up.

"Bill and Ben, why are you playing here?" asked Edward.

"We're *not* playing," protested Bill.

"We're rescuing our trucks," squeaked Ben. "Even *you* don't take our trucks without asking, Edward, but this diseasel did."

"Diseasel? There is no cause to be rude," said Edward, firmly. "This engine is a Metropolitan Vickers Diesel-Electric, Type 2."

The twins wished they hadn't teased the big diesel engine. "We're sorry, Mr – er . . ." said Bill.

"Never mind," the diesel smiled. "Call me BoCo. I'm sorry I didn't understand about the trucks."

"That's better," said Edward. "Now buzz off, you two! Fetch BoCo's trucks – then you can come back for these ones."

Bill and Ben puffed away as fast as their wheels would carry them.

In the Yard, Edward smiled. "Don't worry about those two," he told BoCo, kindly.

"Thank you, Edward," BoCo replied. "I'm glad you were here to keep them in order."

"We call Bill and Ben 'The Bees'. They are terrors when they start buzzing around!" Edward chuckled.

Soon, Bill and Ben came back for their trucks.

This time, they were careful not to be cheeky to BoCo. There was no more teasing and there were no more tricks.

"You *have* been busy bees!" BoCo chuckled.

Edward and BoCo smiled at each other. They were now firm friends.

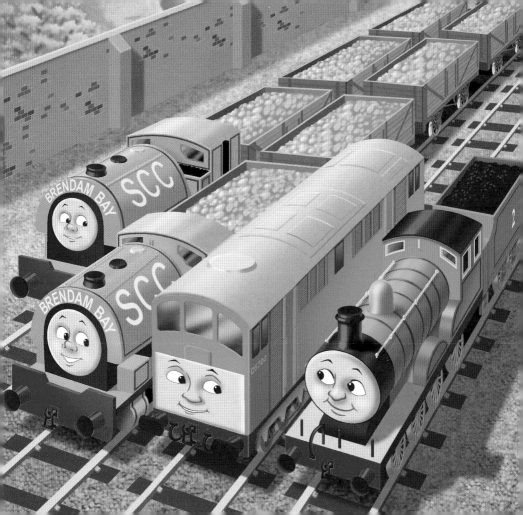

The Thomas Story Library is THE definitive collection of stories about Thomas and ALL his friends.

5 more Thomas Story Library titles will be chuffing into your local bookshop in 2009!

Stanley
Flora
Colin
Hank
Madge

And there are even more Thomas Story Library books to follow late

So go on, add to your Thomas Story Library NOW!

A Fantastic Offer for Thomas the Tank Engine Fans!

In every Thomas Story Library book like this one, you will find a special token. Collect 6 Thomas tokens and we will send you a brilliant Thomas poster, and a double-sided bedroom door hanger! Simply tape a £1 coin in the space above, and fill out the form overleaf.

TO BE COMPLETED BY AN ADULT

To apply for this great offer, ask an adult to complete the coupon below
and send it with a pound coin and 6 tokens, to:
THOMAS OFFERS, PO BOX 715, HORSHAM RH12 5WG

☐ Please send a Thomas poster and door hanger. I enclose 6 tokens
plus a £1 coin. (Price includes P&P)

Fan's name..

Address..

....Postcode...............................

Date of birth...

Name of parent/guardian..

Signature of parent/guardian..

Please allow 28 days for delivery. Offer is only available while stocks last. We reserve the right to change
the terms of this offer at any time and we offer a 14 day money back guarantee. This does not affect your
statutory rights.

☐ Data Protection Act: If you do not wish to receive other similar offers from us or companies we
recommend, please tick this box. Offers apply to UK only.